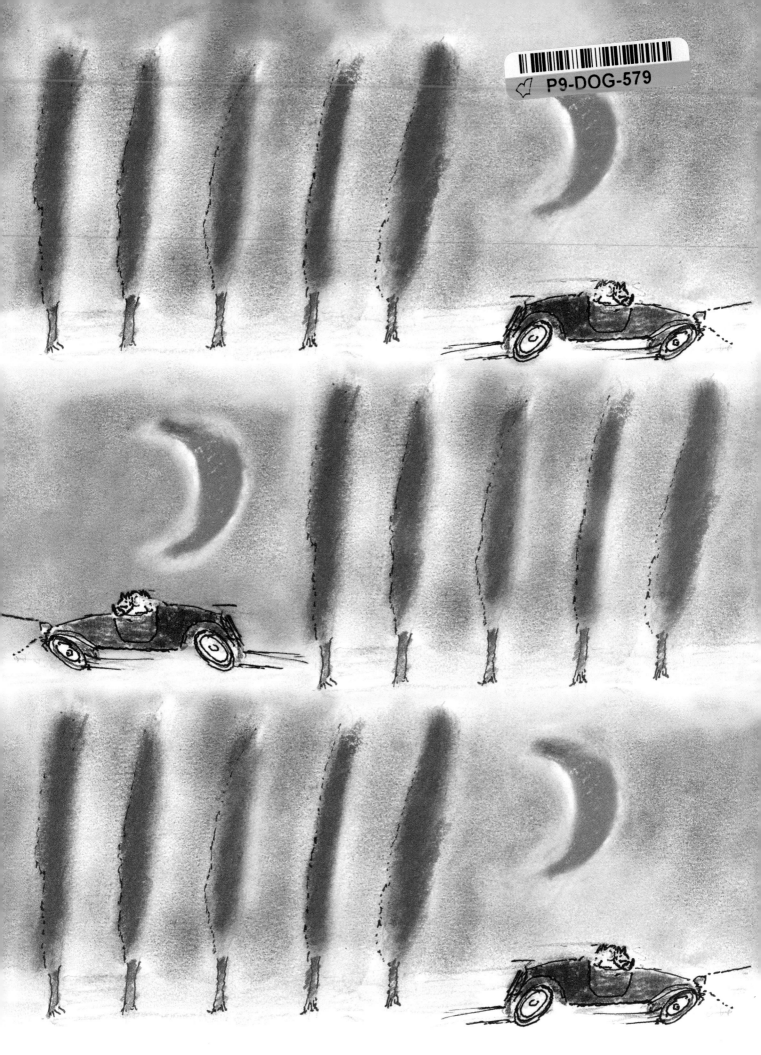

John Burningham
Motor Miles

CANDLEWICK PRESS

Miles, our
much-loved,
difficult dog

Published in Great Britain by Jonathan Cape, an imprint of Random House Children's Publishers U.K.
A Penguin Random House Company

First U.S. edition 2016

Library of Congress Catalog Card Number pending
ISBN 978-0-7636-9064-9

16 17 18 19 20 21 TLF 10 9 8 7 6 5 4 3 2 1

Printed in Dongguan, Guangdong, China

This book was typeset in Goudy Old Style.

Candlewick Press
99 Dover Street
Somerville, Massachusetts 02144

visit us at www.candlewick.com

This is Miles.
Miles was given a home by Alice Trudge
and her son, Norman.
But Miles was a very difficult dog.

Miles did not come when he was called,

did not like going for walks,

and did not like his food . . .

or the rain.

He barked too much . . .

and he didn't like other dogs.

Alice Trudge and Norman were very
fond of Miles, even though he was difficult.

What Miles really liked was to go for
a ride in the car up the hill to the café.

At the café, people said,
"Oh, what a lovely dog."

"I can't go on day after day taking the dog out in the car just to please him," said Alice Trudge.

"What your dog needs is his own car,"
said Mr. Huddy, the man who lived next door.
  "How can I possibly get a car for the dog?"
said Alice Trudge.
  "I will make a car for Miles," said Mr. Huddy.

So Mr. Huddy started to make the car for Miles. And every day after school, Miles and Norman would go to see the car being made.

Finally, Mr. Huddy finished the car
and it was ready for Miles.

"We will have to give you driving lessons," said Mr. Huddy to Miles.

Miles practiced going right,

going left,

and going backward.

Quick STOP!

After many lessons, Miles had learned to
drive and was ready to go on the road.

One morning Alice Trudge could not take Norman to school and did not know what to do.

"I could squeeze into Miles's car and he could take me to school," said Norman.

When Norman arrived at school in a car driven by a dog, all the other children were amazed.

After that Norman and Miles began to go on secret little trips in the car.

One day they went to the seaside very early in the morning.

Other mornings they would drive out
into the countryside.

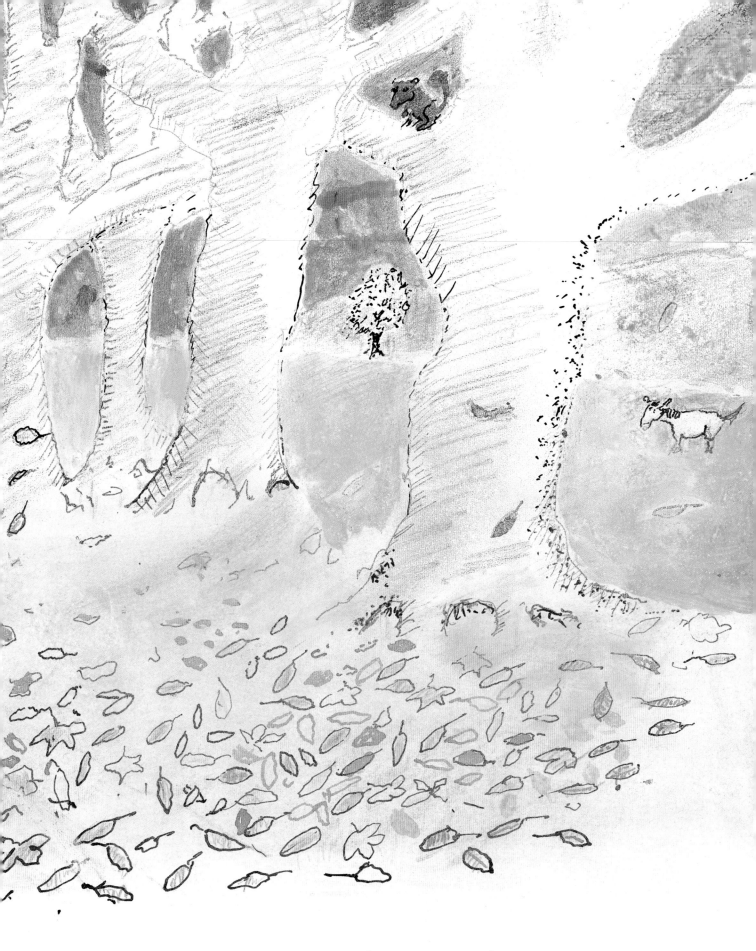

They drove through leaves in the autumn.

And once, in the winter, they drove out
and played in the snow.

Miles was getting easier.

He liked walks,

 his food,

and other dogs.

He didn't mind the rain,

barked less,

and came when he was called.

But Norman was growing up and getting bigger, and soon he could no longer fit in the car.

Miles stopped driving; maybe he didn't like being on his own. So the car was put away.

One day Miles and Norman heard a lot of noise coming from Mr. Huddy's workshop.

"Let's go and see what Mr. Huddy is up to now," said Norman.

Mr. Huddy was starting to make an airplane.

I wonder who that is for?

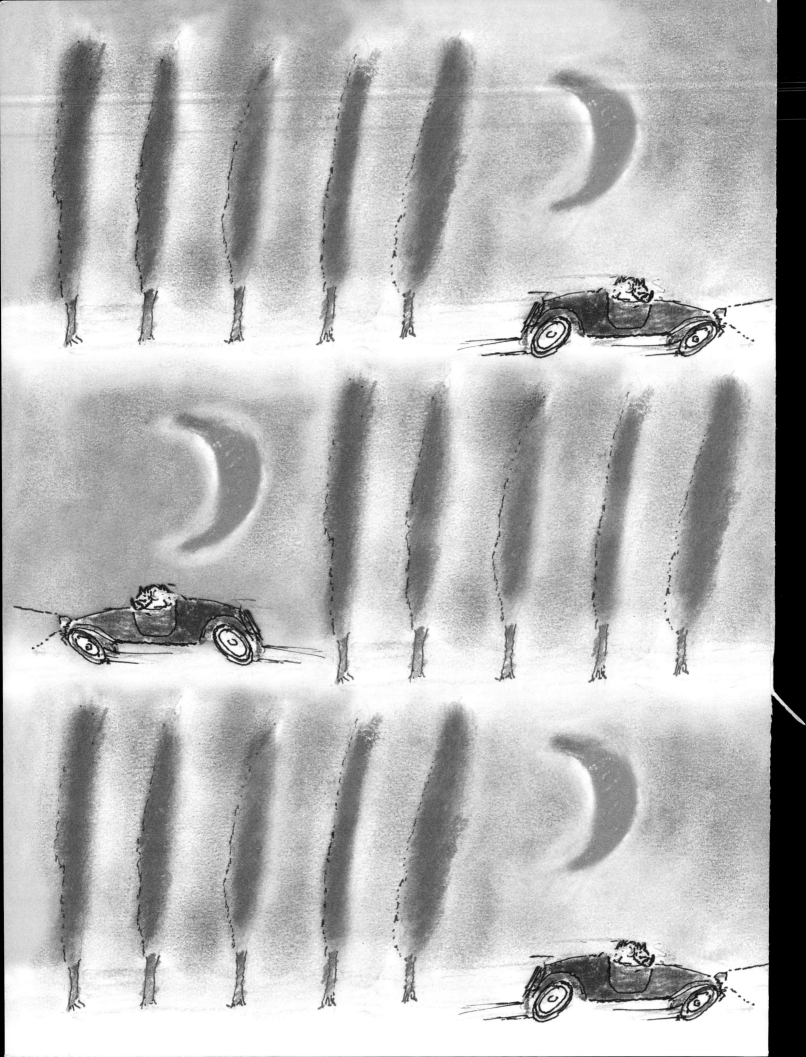